THE VINGANANEE
AND
THE TREE TOAD

A LIBERIAN TALE

RETOLD BY **VERNA AARDEMA** WITH ILLUSTRATIONS BY **ELLEN WEISS**

VIKING KESTREL

To Ken—E.W.

To Sue Benson,
Medical Technician at ELWA Hospital,
Monrovia, Liberia—V.A.

THE VINGANANEE AND THE TREE TOAD is retold
from "Try Your Strength" in a pamphlet, SPIDER
AND OTHER STORIES, by Aunt Clara, Radio Station
ELWA, Monrovia, Liberia, West Africa.

Book Design by Lucy Martin Bitzer and Barbara Du Pree Knowles

VIKING KESTREL
Published by the Penguin Group
Viking Penguin Inc., 40 West 23rd Street, New York, New York 10010, U.S.A.
Penguin Books Ltd, 27 Wrights Lane, London W8 5TZ England
Penguin Books Australia Ltd, Ringwood, Victoria, Australia
Penguin Books Canada Ltd, 2801 John Street, Markham, Ontario, Canada L3R 1B4
Penguin Books (N.Z.) Ltd, 182–190 Wairau Road, Auckland 10, New Zealand

Penguin Books Ltd, Registered Offices: Harmondsworth, Middlesex, England

First published in 1983 by Frederick Warne & Co., Inc.
Re-issued in 1988 by Viking Penguin Inc.
Text copyright © Verna Aardema, 1983
Illustrations copyright © Ellen Weiss, 1983
All rights reserved

The Vingananee and the Tree Toad is retold from "Try Your Strength" in a pamphlet, *Spider and Other Stories*,
by Aunt Clara, Radio Station ELWA, Monrovia, Liberia, West Africa.

ISBN 0-670-82277-9

Printed in the United States of America by Lake Book/Cuneo, Melrose Park, Illinois
Set in Korinna
1 2 3 4 5 92 91 90 89 88

THE VINGANANEE AND THE TREE TOAD

ong ago, when animals talked and lived like people, Spider bought a big farm. It was too big. So he hired Lion and Buck Deer to work for him. They all lived together in Spider's house.

Spider hired a rat to cook for them. Rat was a fine cook. He was neat, t[...] He kept the house all cle[...]

Every day Spider and his men
would go to work on the farm.

At night they would come home and eat the fine stew Rat had cooked.

Then they would lie down.
And the tree toad, who lived in the yard,
would sing them to sleep:

> *Taw-aw-aw-aw-awt,*
> *Taw-aw-aw-aw-awt,*
> *Taw-aw-aw-aw-awt.*

But one day something bad happened!

Spider and the men were at work on the farm. Rat made the stew. Then he was sweeping the floor, *fras, fras, fras,* when he heard someone coming.

Rat looked out the door. There came a strange animal. He looked like one big black, bushy tail. He was coming down the path, *pusu, pusu, pusu.*

Rat couldn't see any feet. He could barely see eyes or a
mouth—but the thing was singing:
"I'm the Vingananee,
And I am hungry.
Give me your stew,
Or I will eat you!"

Rat took the broom and went to
meet him. "How-do, my friend," he said.
"Where do you think you will go?"

"Into your house to eat that stew I
smell cooking," said the Vingananee.

"You will not do it!" said the rat.

"Who will stop me?" said the
Vingananee.

Then, *zaak!* Rat hit the
Vingananee with the broom.
That started a terrible fight,
which the Vingananee won.

And he dragged Rat behind
the house and tied him up,
kpong, kpong, kpong.

Then he went into the house and
ate the stew, *yatua, yatua, yatua*.

When Spider and the men came home from the farm, they were hot and tired and hungry. They looked in the house—no rat! They looked in the cooking pot—no stew!

Spider called, "Rat, where are you? I can't put my eyes on you! Where are you?"

From behind the house they heard *yee, yee, yee*.
They looked, and there was Rat. He was all beaten up.
He was all tied up. He was looking rough!

Spider asked, "Rat, what happened? Who did this to you?"

"The Vingananee. That's who!" said the rat.

"The Vingananee! Who's that?" said the spider.

Rat said, "He looked like one big black, bushy tail. I couldn't see any feet. I could barely see eyes or a mouth. But the thing was singing:

> 'I'm the Vingananee,
> And I am hungry.
> Give me your stew,
> Or I will eat you!'"

Buck Deer snorted, *puh!* "He did eat the stew, too!" he said. "I'm big. I'm tough. Tomorrow I will keep the house. If that Vingananee comes, I will kick him with my feet, *kunch, kunch, kunch!*"

They all felt better then. They untied Rat. They went into the house. They cooked. They ate. They lay down.

And the tree toad sang them to sleep:

Taw-aw-aw-aw-awt,

Taw-aw-aw-aw-awt,

Taw-aw-aw-aw-awt.

When dawn lighted the doorway, Spider and
the men went to work on the farm. Buck Deer
made the stew. Then he was sweeping the floor,
fras, fras, fras, when he heard someone coming.

Buck Deer looked out the door. Down the path came the Vingananee, *pusu, pusu, pusu.* He was singing:

"I'm the Vingananee,
And I am hungry.
Give me your stew,
Or I will eat you!"

Then, *zaak*! Buck Deer hit
the Vingananee with the broom.
That started a terrible fight,
which the Vingananee won.

Buck Deer took the broom and went to
meet him. "My man, where do you think you
will go?" he asked.

"Into your house to eat that stew I smell
cooking," said the Vingananee.

"You will not do it!" said the deer.

"Who will stop me?" said the Vingananee.

And he dragged Buck Deer behind the house and tied him up, *kpong, kpong, kpong.*

Then he went into the house and ate the stew, *yatua, yatua, yatua.*

When Spider and the men returned from the farm, they looked in the house—no Buck Deer! They looked in the cooking pot—no stew! They looked behind the house, and there was Buck Deer. He was all tied up just like Rat had been!

Spider asked, "My man, what happened?"

"You see how I am," said the deer. "The Vingananee did this to me!"

Spider threw up his hands. "What to do!" he cried.

Then Lion roared, *hunn*! "I'm the king of all the animals," he said. "Tomorrow I will keep the house. If that Vingananee comes, I will kill him DEAD!"

They all felt better then. They untied Buck Deer. They went into the house. They cooked. They ate. They lay down.

And the tree toad sang them to sleep:

Taw-aw-aw-aw-awt,

Taw-aw-aw-aw-awt,

Taw-aw-aw-aw-awt.

When dawn lighted the doorway, Spider and the men went to work on the farm. Lion made the stew. Then he was sweeping the floor, *fras, fras, fras,* when he heard someone coming.

Lion looked out the door. Down the path came
the Vingananee, *pusu, pusu, pusu.* He was singing:
"I'm the Vingananee,
And I am hungry.
Give me your stew,
Or I will eat you!"
Lion took the broom and went to meet him. "My
man," he said, "where do you think you will go?"
"Into your house to eat that stew I smell cooking,"
said the Vingananee.
"You will not do it!" said the lion.
"Who will stop me?" said the Vingananee.

Then, *zaak!* Lion hit the Vingananee
with the broom. That started a terrible fight, which
the Vingananee won.

And he dragged Lion behind
the house and tied him up,
kpong, kpong, kpong.

Then he went into the house and
ate the stew, *yatua, yatua, yatua.*

When Spider and the men returned from the farm, they looked
in the house—no Lion! They looked in the cooking pot—no stew!

They were surprised. They couldn't believe something bad had
happened to Lion. But they looked behind the house, and there was
Lion, all tied up just as the others had been.

Spider threw up his hands. "What to do!" he cried.

Buck Deer looked at Spider. "Spider, you're next," he said.

"No. Not me!" cried Spider. "I'm too small. If I keep the house, the Vingananee will eat the stew. Then he'll eat me!"

Now Tree Toad observed all this from a nearby tree. She came over, *lop, lop, lop.* "Tomorrow I will keep the house," she said.

The animals laughed, *gug, gug, gug.*

And Spider said, "Tree Toad, you're small like me. How can you fight the Vingananee?"

"I can try," said Tree Toad.

So they untied Lion. They went into the house. They cooked. They ate. They lay down. And the tree toad sang them to sleep:

Taw-aw-aw-aw-awt,
Taw-aw-aw-aw-awt,
Taw-aw-aw-aw-awt.

When dawn lighted the doorway, Spider and the men set out for the farm. But first, they said good-bye to Tree Toad.

Buck Deer said, "Good-bye, Tree Toad. You've been one good friend."

Lion said, "Good-bye, Tree Toad. We will miss you."

And Spider said, "Good-bye, Tree Toad. We will miss your song."

But they went, anyway.

And Tree Toad made the stew. Then she was sweeping the floor, *fras, fras, fras,* when she heard someone coming. She looked out the door.

Down the path came the Vingananee,
pusu, pusu, pusu. He was singing:
　　"I'm the Vingananee,
　　And I am hungry.
　　Give me your stew,
　　Or I will eat you!"

Tree Toad took the broom. She stood in the middle of the path. She said, "How-do, my friend. Where do you think you will go?"

That Vingananee didn't answer! He didn't even slow down. He just came faster, *pusu, pusu, pusu, pusu.*

He grabbed Tree Toad and threw her into the air.
The broom went one way and Tree Toad the other.
But when she came down, she didn't get hurt,
because tree toads can bounce, *pomm, pomm.*

But the Vingananee
caught her and
threw her up again!

 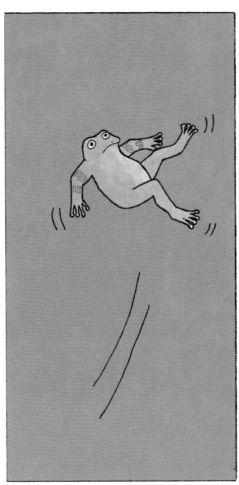 

He did this again,   and again,   and again!

At last, Tree Toad
couldn't stand any more.
She looked up at the sky
and said, "God, you made me so I don't get hurt
when I fall. I thank you for that. But I can't fight
this Vingananee. You must help me."

Then, next time the Vingananee threw Tree Toad up, he made a bad mistake! He threw her straight up—so high, she was almost gone. When she came down, she fell, *twum,* right on the Vingananee's head!

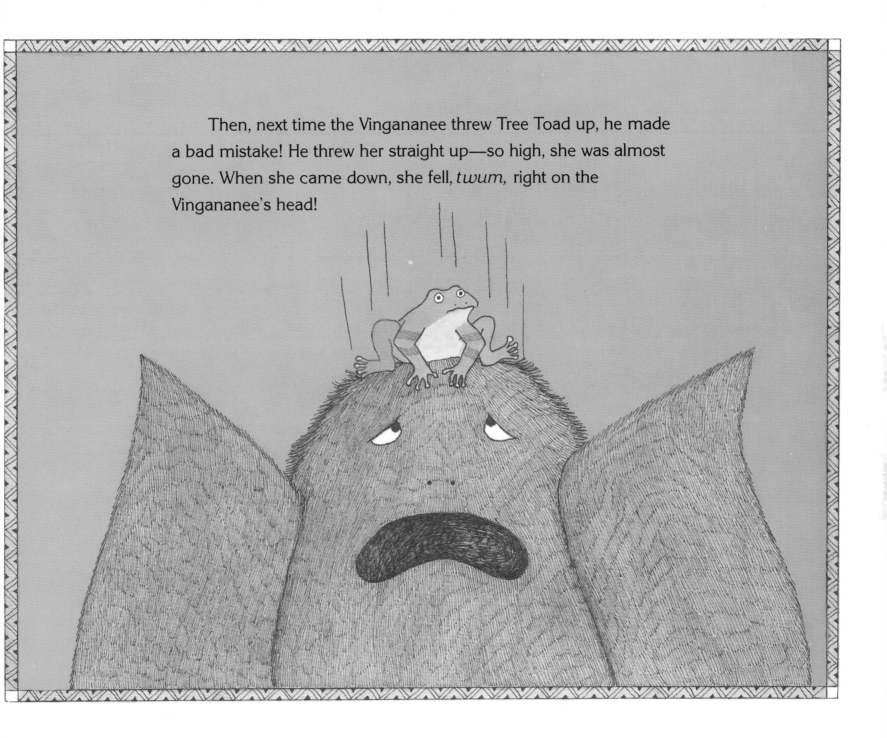

The Vingananee fell over, *twaaa*, and lay still.

Tree Toad was surprised. But she was not sure that the Vingananee was really dead. So, *lop, lop, lop,* she went. She fetched the rope, and tied up the Vingananee right there on the path, *kpong, kpong, kpong.*

Then she sat down to wait.

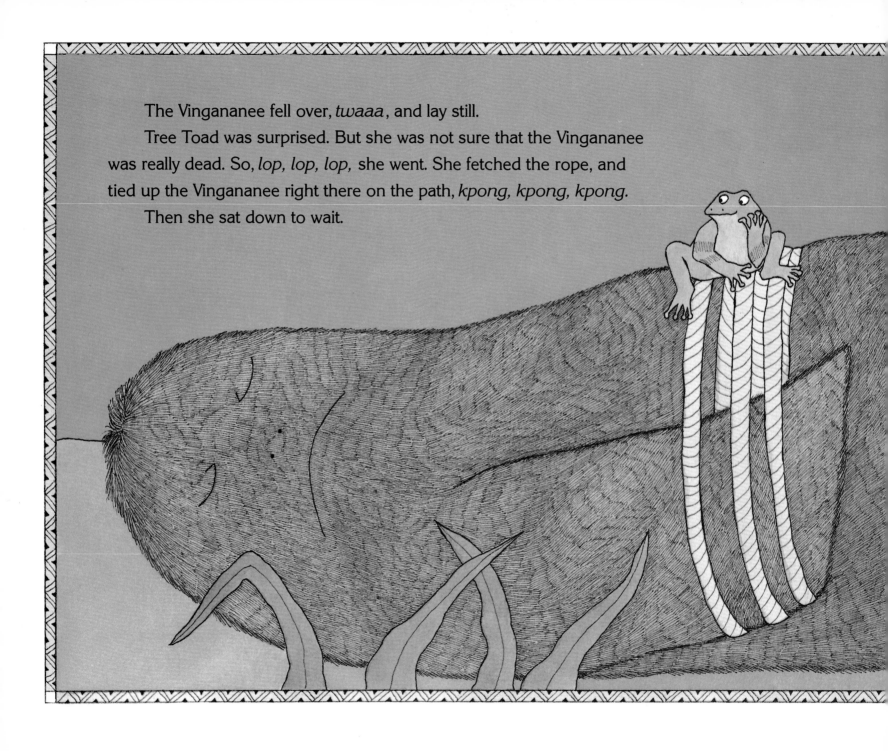

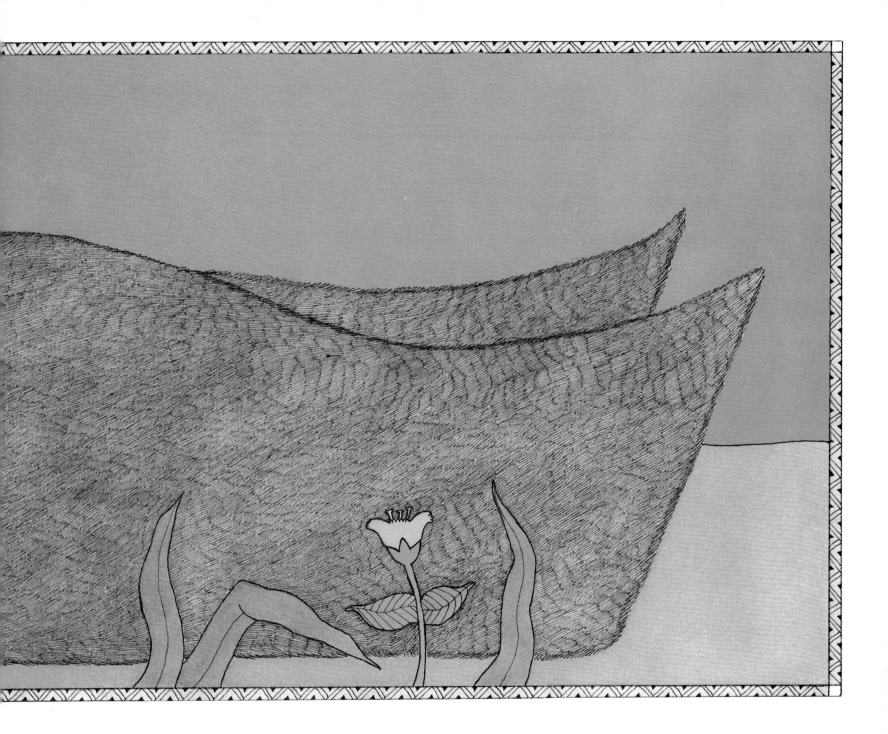

That evening, Spider and the men were sad as they returned from the farm. They expected to find Tree Toad dead. But when they drew near the house, they saw the Vingananee all tied up on the path.

And there was Tree Toad—very much alive—sitting beside him!

Spider said, "Tree Toad, how did you fight the Vingananee? How did you win?"

Tree Toad spread her small green fingers wide. "It was a miracle!" she cried.

The End

This book is dedicated to the memory of Aunt Clara who told her version of this tale to the children of West Africa, many years ago. Aunt Clara was an African Storyteller, but she didn't tell tales under the moon in a village plaza. She told them on her Kiddies' Korner Program over Radio ELWA, in the modern city of Monrovia, Liberia.

Aunt Clara, whose full name was Mrs. Clara Letitia Blaine-Wilson, was an Americo-Liberian. That means she was a descendant of freed American slaves who had returned to Africa. When she was about to enter the sixth grade,

Clara was taken to America to finish her education. Later, she returned to Africa as a teacher and taught in an academy, a community school, and at the College of West Africa. For 22 years she was the children's storyteller at ELWA Radio Station.

Aunt Clara was so highly regarded by the government of Liberia, that when she died on August 9, 1979, she was given a state funeral. Flags were flown at half mast. The late President William R. Tolbert, Jr., attended the services, and the army and police bands played.